. *Dancing Carl* .

DANCING CARL

by Gary Paulsen

◆ ◆ ◆ ◆

Bradbury Press   *Scarsdale, N.Y.*

Bradbury Press, Inc.
2 Overhill Road
Scarscale, N.Y. 10583
An affiliate of Macmillan, Inc.
Collier Macmillan Canada, Inc.
Manufactured in the United States of America
10 9 8 7 6 5 4 3 2 1
Library of Congress Cataloging in Publication Data
Paulsen, Gary.
Dancing Carl.
Summary: Two boys "hero worship" a man they are told to stay
away from.
I. Title.
PZ7.P2843Dan   1983   [Fic]   83-2663
ISBN 0-02-770210-3

To R. J.

. : I : .

In the summer, in McKinley, Minnesota, when you are twelve there is so much to do that almost none of it gets done except fishing.

It isn't that McKinley is big, or busy. It's only got twelve hundred people—not much more than when my great-grandfather Marshall Knuteson homesteaded the town site. I was named after him and everybody calls me Marsh except Willy who is my best friend and always just says *hey* when he wants me. He also says there are only nine hundred people in town but Kayo Morgan who owns the grocery says there are more to attract tourists.

I have never figured out why having more people would bring tourists in but I don't own a grocery, either, so there it is. But it's not a big town.

And there's no real business either except some logging in the winter when the swamps are frozen enough to skid the big logs out of the woods. Also there are a few farms but they're small because of the dampness in the soil which turns to mud in the spring during planting. The mud sticks the tractors so bad they have to use work teams of horses to pull them out and what with running back and forth with horses to pull tractors out you really couldn't call it farming. So you couldn't call McKinley a busy town, either.

But in the summer, for some reason, all the get-done things seem to come at you. The yard needs raking down and mowing with the push mower. Dad doesn't like the rotary power mowers because they rip rather than cut. The garden needs weeding—*all* the time—the back yard fence needs mending and tightening because Willy Taylor's pony can't stand to stay out of new corn and leans on the wire. Trash needs to be burned and the front fence needs painting or the rot takes the wood and the flower beds need cleaning from the cats and the storm windows have to come down and the screens go up or the mosquitos carry you off and, and, and . . .

It doesn't have to be a big town or a busy town to keep you jumping in the summer. And then, right in the middle, to make it worse Willy Taylor comes by and he's got his rod over his shoulder and some night crawlers and angleworms in an old cottage cheese carton and that pretty much takes care of finishing whatever chore you're doing.

Willy has a way of talking so you think just ahead of what he's saying. He'll stop by the yard when I'm mowing the grass and he'll stare down the street with his shoulders kind of over and down the way he has of standing, holding the rod in one hand and the worms in the other. Then he'll smile and say, "The grass won't grow much between now and dark."

And what he really means is that the fish are biting and while you can always mow a lawn the fish aren't always biting.

Out south of town there is an old iron and concrete bridge across the Poplar River. In the spring it runs with suckers, which aren't much good for anything but fertilizer and pet food although some folks smoke them and swear by them.

But in the middle of the summer the water in the Poplar settles down to tame and the suckers head back into the lakes and the mud and the fishing on the bridge gets good if you're serious.

Willy and I live there in the summer, or so it seems. Every afternoon we try to get down there, or almost every afternoon.

Using a small hook and a piece of worm you

slide the hook down gently alongside the concrete pilings, right along the edge of the cement. That's where the big rock bass wait and if you use a light line and light leader it can be fun catching them. They're scrappy. But it's even more fun eating them when they're battered in egg and cornmeal and fried just past moist in a hot pan the way my mother cooks them.

Sometimes we sit in the summer sun down there all day. There's hardly any traffic on the bridge because it leads out to farms and farmers don't come into town that much. It can be pretty private and when Willy gets to talking it's fun to feel the sun and just listen with one finger on the line waiting for that raspy feeling that means a rock bass is mouthing the bait, sucking it in and out the way they do before they take it.

It was on a summer day like that with us down at the bridge fishing that the story of Carl started, even though Carl is all winter and ice. Or part of the story anyway.

It was hot and they weren't biting but it didn't matter. The sun was keeping the mosquitos down and we had our shirts off getting tanned and Willy snorted.

"You know, McKinley isn't like other towns."

Considering that Willy was like me and neither one of us had ever lived anywhere except McKinley it hit me that Willy couldn't know what other towns were like but I kept my mouth shut. If you got set to argue with Willy you had to make sure you had some big guns. It wasn't that he was always right, though he usually was—it was that he read so much that even when he was wrong he could throw in so much extra stuff that you felt lucky to get a word in. So I didn't say anything, but I thought it. I knew he'd go on anyway.

"It's the grownups," he continued. "In McKinley the grownups are different."

Well. I couldn't let that one go by. "How could you know that? And how are they different?"

Willy held up his hand for silence and stared at his line as if he had a bite but I knew he was just thinking, buying time.

"I read a lot, that's how I know," he said after a moment. "In McKinley people are kind of old-fashioned. Take your dad, for instance."

"My dad?" Actually my parents are probably the least old-fashioned people in McKinley. Dad even talked about getting an Edsel. "My dad isn't old-fashioned."

"Sure he is. Doesn't he stick with that old push mower instead of changing over to the new rotary kind?"

Like I say, Willy always comes out on top. "That's not so old-fashioned."

"Sure it is. And the rest of McKinley is like that. There are lots of people in town who still use the old push mowers. They rebuild them and

5

keep them going. And they take care of their own families, too."

There was a jump, I thought—from push mowers to families. "How does that make them old-fashioned?"

"They don't let the state do it, like everybody else in the country. They take care of their own. And from what I read, that's pretty old-fashioned . . ."

And I think he was going to say more but he got the rasp that meant a bite then and when the bass took the hook he set it and landed it and the rest of the afternoon was spent fishing.

But what he was talking about McKinley being old-fashioned became part of Carl's story because Carl was one of those people the town sort of took care of themselves rather than let the state do it. Or at least that's how it started and went until it all turned around and Carl took care of the town. Or at least the rinks.

The rinks.

In the summer everything just splashes out, out into warm days and warm nights and mosquitos and some rain and sun and taking Willy's cousin's canoe down the Poplar camping until there isn't any summer left and nothing really to remember except a kind of warm feeling of fun and no real purpose.

But in the winter there are the rinks, only the rinks and hockey and skating and that is all. Unless you count school, which is more or less just always there. But there isn't anything else to do in McKinley in the winter and the rinks become a central place in town.

In the winter people who were off on summer vacations come back and everybody meets at the rinks and everything that was loose and unorganized becomes tighter. Winter does that to everything in northern Minnesota—brings it in.

But for the people in town the rinks do more than just organize, they become the winter part of the town that means everything. The rinks *are* the town in the winter, even for the grownups, and that's what made Carl so important.

That's why when Carl came to the rinks and danced and fell in love with Helen and moved so only Helen and some of the kids could understand at first, that's why it affected the whole town.

The rinks are everything in the winter. And that winter Dancing Carl became everything at the rinks and taught us about living and being what we were and loving all mixed into the cold and ice-blue flat of the skating rinks.

It was some of it a sad time and some of it a very happy time and a lot more of it a hurting time but most of all, like Willy Taylor said when it was all over, it was the best time there ever was to be twelve moving towards thirteen.

. : 2 : .

In the summer the rinks are a dirt parking lot
for tourists who are too tired to drive on through
McKinley to get to the good tourist places up
north. It isn't much. Just a gravel pad down off
the main street at the north end of town next to
Pederson's Hardware—which is really Johnson's
Hardware but has always been called Pederson's for the original owner. Old man Pederson
was a shirttail cousin or great-third uncle to me
but I never knew him. He left before I was born.

The town more or less keeps the gravel level
and now and then people driving through who
want a short rest will stop. But there is nothing
to keep them—all the good muskie fishing is up
north—and they always leave after a few hours.
Of course they don't know about the rock bass

at the bridge, but that's for the best—they'd just fish it out.

On the east side of the area there are a couple of wooden outdoor bathrooms, pretty well kept up and smelling of strong lime all the time. Cully Fransen is the caretaker in the summer and he's a good worker even if he doesn't think straight all the time and has to stay in when it rains or snows. He's not old but something is burned out in his brain and they keep him on in the summer and pay him a little something. I'm not sure what happened but it was something to do with some pills his mother took before he was born.

I asked Dad about Cully one time at supper and he looked at me for a long time before answering.

"He has the mind of a four-year-old," Dad said, "in most areas. But he is an adult in some ways and can live a useful life. Why this sudden interest in Cully Fransen?"

"Oh, no real reason." Dad has a way of looking at you sometimes so even if you haven't done anything wrong you try to remember if you ever *did* do something wrong. "We were just walking by there the other day and saw him working in the park and I thought I'd ask about him."

"You weren't studying on teasing him or anything, were you?"

I shook my head. Some people had done that,

teased Cully some, but I hadn't. It just didn't seem right. "I was just curious. I see him there all summer, each day, and I wondered."

Dad nodded. "Curiosity is a good thing—it leads to education." Dad believed in education because he didn't get so much because he had to work on grandpa's farm. "With Cully the township board met and decided it would be better to give him some work and a room and a little money. Better than sending him to a state institution."

"Doesn't he have any family?"

"Not anymore. He did, he had a mother, but she took legs some time back."

"What do you mean, 'took legs'?"

Dad studied me for a moment and then shook his head. "Not yet. Maybe later we'll get into that . . ."

And I was going to ask more about it but Mom came in with supper then and we tucked in.

But Cully took good care of the park area in the summer, kept it clean and raked down. Which was good because the gravel parking area was really the rinks, in the winter.

On the other side from the bathrooms, on the west side of the gravel area, there is a wooden building—actually a shack—which is closed in the summer and used for a warming house in the winter.

All around the parking lot there are elm trees. They are huge and scraggly with thin leaves in the summer and no leaves in the late fall and the winter. But in a way they look nice, too—like they belong to the place, or hold it in like arms.

Willy once told me that if he grew up without getting dumb somehow he was going to become an artist and come back and paint those elms. But when I asked him where he was going to come back from he didn't know except that it was going to be across an ocean so I wouldn't count on it. Willy sometimes gets a little excited about things that other people don't even notice.

But the elms are pretty, just the same, and in the winter they hold the four torn old speakers which hang around the rinks to make waltz music for the Saturday night skate-dancing the grownups do. The elms kind of fit that music, all scratchy and warbly, and they aren't bad to see even if they're ugly and scraggly, too.

Nothing ever happens on the gravel in the summer. Oh, once Dennis Hendricks who is the town constable had a fight there with four mean motorcycle guys who were coming through. But they left when Dennis got mad and thumped one of them so bad his ears bled out—Dennis being built big and roughly square and awfully strong.

But other than that the summers are pretty boring down where the rinks are.

In the fall there comes a time when everybody in town gets a kind of strange feeling. It comes just after the first hard frost, in October, and gets more and more in the open as the fall hardens.

Part of it is a reaction to winter coming, and part of it is a reaction to summer going. Willy says it comes from the people being sick of the summer mug-heat that comes late and the bad last days of mosquitos and maybe he's right.

The main thing is that the feeling comes and the leaves drop and there comes a day in November when all the people in town gather down at the gravel of the rink pad and they bring rakes and shovels and spend the day leveling and cleaning.

This is not something that is planned. I never saw a word pass or anybody talk about it. One day it all just works and we all go down and rake and clean. Then we put up the board walls around where the two rinks will be. These are wooden walls stored in the basement of the town hall—a big building in back of the hardware.

The walls lock together with wooden boards which are nailed into position and when it's all together there are two large wooden ovals with kind of square corners sitting on the gravel pad—long way north and south, right next to the warming house. Once the walls are up, all nicked and scarred with puck marks, then some posts are put on top of the walls between the two rinks and chicken wire mesh is raised to stop pucks. The west rink is for general use, counterclockwise skating and figure skating in the middle. But the east rink is for hockey, which goes on all the time and gets rough and the chicken wire is absolutely necessary to keep the puck from shooting across and taking somebody's teeth out, which happened with Mary-Jo Kinsky before they put the wire up. Richard Erickson made a wild slap shot and the puck went just over the board and hit Mary-Jo full on in the mouth and it was an awful mess.

When the rinks are all done, and the wire is up and tightened and the gravel pads are raked and reraked and the nights are cold but the sun cooks the days, the waiting starts.

Everybody in town waits. And maybe it isn't just for the rinks, but for the coming of winter, because even those people who don't skate seem to be waiting. They look out windows, they look up at the sky when they're out walking—they wait. And if it is for the winter and not for skating it doesn't matter because it's the same thing. They might as well be waiting on the rinks because in a way the rinks mean winter.

Everybody waits. The warming house is cleaned out and the two bathrooms relimed and painted inside to remove the wall writing and we wait. The problem is that it's too soon to flood the rinks because the water will thaw in the day when the sun hits it. Without hard freeze it just keeps sinking into the gravel and the waiting is very hard to do because everybody is ready to start skating.

Start winter, start skating, start getting down to the business of winter—that's how Willy says it.

"Summer is fun, summer is fishing," he said in the summer before Carl. We were down by the power dam trying to snag sheepsheads to sell to the mink farmer south of town for a quarter each. Sometimes you could get twenty or thirty of them and even if snagging wasn't quite the right way to fish everybody wanted to get rid of the sheepsheads so they didn't care.

"Summer is soft," Willy said. "It's just mush. Everything is easygoing and slow." He stopped long enough to jerk up with the wrist action that set the snag hook in a sheepshead but missed. "Now you want to get down to business, that's winter. Winter is when you get things done."

Which might be why some of the people waited, to get away from the soft of summer and into the hard of winter.

After school the kids and some of the grown-ups go down to the rinks and stand and wait, looking at the gravel, waiting for it to get hard and stay hard. Not all the same people just standing, but people come by. If you stayed there for a couple of hours on a November evening you would likely see just about everybody in town as they came by to check the rinks, maybe to stand a bit, then move on and it was during this time that we first saw Carl.

Or that's when we first remembered seeing Carl although he might have been around for some time before then.

It was in late November, after Thanksgiving, in the end of daylight just before dark. By that time of the year it gets dark around five, and even with the lights strung in the elms next to the speakers most people don't stay much after dark unless they're skating. But this time there was a fair crowd of ten or twelve kids and grownups, standing near the boards, trying to look like they were being natural and Willy nudged me with his elbow and pointed with his chin and there was Carl.

He was sort of old, but not wrinkle-old so much as worn-old or worked-old, and he stood angled over a little with a stoop that looked like it came from tired and maybe something a little more. He didn't have a hat on and his hair was gray and tight and cut short, bushy and thick, and his face was all straight lines.

His eyes were narrow but you could see the

red in them, and there was red on his cheeks and down his straight nose and it was the kind of red that didn't go away even when he came in. It was the kind of red that came from drinking. The kind of red Pisspot Jimmy got when he had been drinking hard.

Carl was wearing an old leather sheepskin flight jacket maybe from the war and it was tattered and all over holes so you could see little bits of the wool lining poking out here and there. The collar was up and he moved his head from side to side a bit to warm first one ear and then the other.

While I was looking at him that first time with Willy he took a bottle in a paper sack out of the right pocket of his flight jacket and took a drink and there was a kind of flowing movement to it all. As if he'd done it a lot. And the bottle came out and up and he took a swig and then back and down into the pocket, like a circle, just up, back and down and nobody else seemed to notice and I thought then, I thought here's a new town drunk for Dennis to take care of but I knew even then somehow that I was wrong.

There was something else in the drinking. Something that made it beautiful and business all at once. It wasn't sloppy, the way Jimmy had been, and he didn't try to hide it the way Jimmy had done, but right out in the open and the bottle was part of him, part of Carl just the way the red was part of Carl and the jacket was part of Carl.

Then, while we watched he climbed over the boards on the side of the east rink and walked into the middle of the gravel pad and knelt down and felt the dirt.

In a moment he stood and walked to another place and did the same, squatting and checking, and this time he stood and nodded.

"Tomorrow. We can flood her tomorrow," he said in a low rasp. He had whiskey throat, just like Jimmy, but there was a strong edge to it so it made you want to look at him and it was in this way that Carl became part of the rinks, part of the town, and came into our lives. It was that simple. He just jumped over the boards and walked into the middle of the gravel and told us it was time to flood the rinks and I held my breath and Willy stiffened.

Deciding when it was time to flood was everybody's decision, even the kids', but it was Stan Johnson who had the final word.

Stan was in charge of the volunteer fire department, ran the truck and took care of the hoses, and water from the hydrant was how the rinks were flooded so Stan had the final say.

I figured there would be trouble because Stan was standing down at the end nearest Carl and he had kind of a flash temper. But Carl looked over to him and there was something that went between them, something at first tight and then more friendly and all without words the trouble passed.

Stan nodded, and smiled, and went off to get hoses ready and some of the others went to help and they left Carl standing in the middle of the dirt of the rink and Willy let his breath out in a rush. I had been holding mine, too, and I took a deep pull.

"Did you see that?" Willy asked. "I mean did you *see* that?"

I nodded.

"It's like he was king or something," he said, whispering. "Like he was king of the rinks."

And I nodded again but I was looking out to where Carl still stood and he took another pull at the bottle in the sack in his pocket and I thought maybe Stan did it out of pity.

Of course that's before I knew about the power that Carl had, the power and the way he had of making things which are normally ugly have a kind of beauty.

That was before I understood anything or had seen Carl make things happen where nothing had happened before. That was before I understood that Carl *was* king of the rinks and maybe a lot more, too.

. : 3 : .

My dad is the kind of dad who makes rules and you live by them. He's never taken a stick to me, unless you count the time when I was small and Willy and I played cavalry charge with Schaeker's chickens down the block and some of the chickens lost. That time he made me cut a switch. But outside of that he hasn't had to switch—but even so there's something about his rules that makes you want to obey them.

One of his rules is that nothing bad or depressing should be talked about at supper. He says it makes the meal go down wrong, makes the food taste bad and it's a rule both Mom and I agree with so we do it. Of course I'd do it even if I didn't agree with him.

But the night after Carl had decided it was

time to flood the rinks I had a problem. On the one hand I wanted to talk to Dad about Carl and the rinks and what we'd seen and on the other hand I wasn't sure if that was something bad.

I still figured maybe Carl was just another town drunk and that might not be the thing to talk about at supper and I took too long to think about it because my fork kind of started pushing some string beans around on my plate.

"What's wrong with your beans?" Mom asked.

"Oh, nothing. I was just thinking."

"Well. Eat your beans."

"Sure." I took a mouthful and chewed but Dad hadn't missed it and he paused in his eating.

"What were you thinking about?"

I finished chewing. That's another rule. Don't talk with food in your mouth. "I'm not really sure if it's right to talk about it at supper."

Dad nodded. "I see. Why don't you tell us the subject and we'll decide."

I thought a minute. "It's about Carl, that new guy down at the rinks today."

"What's the matter with talking about him?"

"He drinks some. Maybe a lot."

"Still, I don't see . . . Oh. You mean he drinks as in alcoholic?"

"Maybe. I don't know for sure."

"Well, go ahead. It should be all right to talk about at supper."

So I told Mom and him about Carl and how it

had been at the rinks and about how Carl had kind of taken the decision away from Stan John-son and when I was done Dad smiled.

"That's very interesting. Stan normally does all the decision making about the rinks and Carl jumped right in, did he?"

I nodded. "And Stan just took it. Who is this guy anyway?"

Dad thought for a long time before answering. "First off, he's isn't a 'guy,' his name is Carl, Carl Wenstrom. He is a man who started years ago in McKinley and went away and had some trou-bles in his life and needs help. Still, that's inter-esting about Stan. I always thought Stan was a little too aggressive—maybe I was wrong."

I knew we were getting close to the edge but I thought I'd try. "What kind of trouble did Carl have?"

Dad hesitated. "He was in the war, the Sec-ond World War, not Korea. Something hap-pened and he needs help. There were many like that who came back and needed help. That's why they hired Carl to take care of the rinks and stay in the warming house—it's the town's way of taking care of him."

"But what kind of trouble?"

"Eat your dinner."

"Yes sir." I took a forkful of string beans be-cause his voice had dropped and gotten that edge that meant we were into the rules area.

But I was a little wrong about Carl and a little right. He drank, but maybe there was a reason for it, the trouble Dad was talking about. And maybe that didn't make it all right to drink but it explained why Stan had backed off. Maybe he was just being nice to Carl.

One time Willy and I were sitting on the edge of the Poplar River in the fall just before school started and we got to talking, the way you do, and I wondered how we would be when we were old.

"How old?" Willy asked.

"Up there. Like maybe thirty or so. What will we be like?"

"We'll be like we are now, only older," he said. "I was reading an article just the other day that said the habits we establish now will be with us the rest of our lives."

"They never change?"

"The article said they didn't. Not unless you forced them."

"You mean Johnny Severson will always drink sideways out of his mouth so he can see what's going on?"

"Yup."

"You read too much." I watched the river go by for a while. "It's not good for you."

"I'm establishing a habit for later."

Which isn't about Carl but shows something about Willy and how he came to know so much about ice. He reads all the time, when he isn't skating or fishing and sometimes he reads while he's fishing. So once when he was reading he came across information about ice and how it forms and during the fall when we first met Carl he told me down by the rinks after school.

It was the day after I had talked to Dad at the supper table and it was just getting dark and we went by the rinks to see how the flooding was going.

Stan Johnson's hoses were laid and the water was running onto the gravel of the rinks, making puddles that would stiffen and freeze as we watched. It layered out and out, heading towards the boards of the sides and it was getting colder as it got closer into hard dark. I was just thinking how good a cup of hot chocolate would taste in the warmth of our kitchen when Willy rubbed his chin and nodded towards the rinks like a wise old man.

"You know," he said slowly, "ice is pretty incredible stuff."

That's how he put it—*incredible stuff*. I mean we're just cutting past twelve and he talks like that. "Just how do you mean that?"

"Well, when you get to know it and how it's formed it doesn't seem like it could be made out of water."

"Of course it's water. That's ridiculous. You hit water with cold and you get ice."

"But it goes through stages," he said, tipping his head so that even though he was a little shorter than me he was kind of talking down to me. "It gets stronger and weaker as it goes, harder and softer, changes crystals and even color. It changes all the time with cold."

I nodded. "I knew that. Everybody up here does. That's why ice talks in the winter." On the river, when the deep cold of midwinter comes, the hard cold of January and February, the ice cracks and moves and makes sounds that come pretty close to talking. Low music, rolling through the ice—close to the sounds the whales make. It scares you at first, especially if you're right on the ice, but when you get used to it there's music in it.

"Some people believe the old stories they tell about the Indians saying the spirits talk through the ice in the winter—I read that somewhere," I finished, so Willy wouldn't think he was the only one who ever read a book. But he wasn't listening to me.

He was looking across the rinks to the warming house where the door opened and Carl came out. It was almost totally dark now and the light framed him in the doorway through the steam coming off the water running out of the hoses.

The outside lights weren't on because Mc-Kinley doesn't waste money and why light the rinks when there aren't any skaters? But there was some light from the street lights, enough to see that Carl was drunk.

Stan was by the hydrant but Carl didn't go over to him. Instead he went to the head of the rinks, near the gate that went onto the general skating rink, and stood with his hands jammed down in his pockets.

"He's checking the ice," Willy said, almost in a whisper, although he could never have been heard over the sound of the running water. "He's making sure it's coming all right."

And maybe he was, even though there was no way Willy could have known that just from seeing Carl standing there. I just thought it was all sort of eerie and strange looking, Carl framed in the steam and the glow from the street lights.

Then he did something neither of us expected. He turned, as if he might be heading back into the warming house, but instead he turned his back to the rinks and raised his arms out to the side, palms flat and down.

Slowly, with his arms out that way, he made a complete circle, looking straight out to the front as he went around. Then he put his arms down and went around again, slower, and up his hands came, way out to the side and I thought they looked like two small birds lifting his arms—fluttering gently, and then down again.

He went back into the warming house. It was completely dark now and we didn't move for a while. Out of the corner of my eye I saw Willy's breath making little gray puffs in the cold-dark air, puffs that moved out and rose and fell just as Carl's hands had done.

"What was that?" Willy said, after a longer time still. It wasn't really a question and I didn't have an answer anyway so I didn't say anything.

"It was so strange," he said in another minute. "So strange a thing to do."

I nodded. "Kind of pretty though."

"Yeah. But strange—I wonder what it meant?"

"Why does it have to mean something?"

"Because." Willy stopped, looked back at the warming house and began to walk again. We had started moving for home and since Willy lived close by my house it was the same way. "Because everything has to mean something. There is nothing that doesn't mean something."

I chewed on that for a while, walking through the cold. "What about the time old Sarah Goodman took to talking backwards and the words didn't mean anything?"

But in Willy's brain there was nothing without sense and he couldn't be beaten down. "That meant that she was old and broken. She'd had a stroke—that's what it meant."

"So maybe Carl is old and broken. Or crazy." I said it fast but I knew it was wrong when I said it. Carl was neither really old nor broken, just different, and Willy didn't bother to answer and we walked the rest of the way home in silence.

When I went to bed I dropped to sleep right away, the way I always do when the weather starts to turn cold and the ice is forming. But after a little time I snapped awake and sat up and was looking at the wall and didn't know why except that when I lay back down on the pillow and started down into sleep again I thought of Carl.

Nothing more than that.

Just thought of Carl and then down into sleep where I dreamt of the rinks—without Carl—and hockey and I won and won.

· ∶ 4 ∶ ·

In the winter school was usually something we got through, waiting to hit the rinks. But sometimes in the fall, between when they started to flood the rinks and when we could get on the ice—which seemed to take a year—sometimes school was all we had.

Willy is good at it, good at school. Sometimes he even knows more than the teachers because of the way he reads all the time. But I have to work at getting things. They come, but it seems to take sweat and now and then I have to work it over twice before it sticks. Especially math and science. And Willy just slicks through it so easy it would make you sick to see it.

Still, hard or not when there isn't any ice yet all there is comes to being school and in a backward way school helped us to understand Carl, or if not understand him see him a little better, see him the way he was supposed to be seen, or at least that's what Willy said, later when the dancing ended.

It was funny, how it happened. We hadn't really seen Carl yet but Miss Johnson who was so pretty it was hard not to stare and Willy stared anyway—Miss Johnson was in the hallway talking to Mr. Melonowski who taught social studies and coached the football team and Willy and I were in the hall coat closet where we couldn't be seen but could hear it all.

"We could meet somewhere," Mr. Melonowski said to her. "We have to meet somewhere. I have to talk to you."

"No. I don't think so. You're married." Miss Johnson's voice didn't sound like she meant the no very much and I poked Willy hard with my elbow and made a funny face but he signed me to shut up.

"I don't think we should meet," Miss Johnson said again. "I really don't think we should . . ."

And they moved away and maybe none of it would have mattered except that later, on the way home, we started talking.

"It comes to being in love," Willy said. He had stopped to look down at an anthill in the sidewalk. Here it was, coming into winter, and the sun was out and an ant came out and went back down into the hole.

"You mean in the hall." I squatted to see the ant better but it didn't come out again. "Melon and Miss Johnson."

"Yes. That comes down to being in love."

I thought about it. "I don't think so. I don't know for sure what you'd call it but I know it isn't love." The ant still hadn't come up. He might not come up until spring, now, until all that winter time had gone. Earlier in the day we had been talking about love and I thought that the way I felt about Shirley Winge was love and I said it but Willy had stopped me.

"That's not love. We're too young to feel love."

"I don't believe that. When I look at her my knees hurt and I get a stomachache and that's got to be awfully close to love."

And now Willy was talking about Melonowski and Miss Johnson and called it love. "I don't know," I said. "I don't know if Melon's knees hurt."

"Ahh, you don't know anything. Let's go to the rinks and see if the ice is ready."

Of course later we saw what real love was, saw how it could take a man and a woman, saw how it could take Carl. And maybe because of school we got an idea of something to compare it to when we saw it.

But all of that came later.

When we got to the rinks Stan Johnson was coiling up the hoses and putting them back onto the truck.

The ice was ready.

When Stan finished he looked up at us and smiled. "You can skate now. But she'll be a little soft until we get hard cold."

We nodded. We didn't have our skates and couldn't skate until we'd gone home for them but before we could leave Carl came out of the warming house and walked to the rinks.

He stood, looking out across the ice for a full minute, maybe more, stiff and straight, then he pulled the bottle out of his pocket and looked over the top of us.

"Not yet. Tomorrow."

"But Stan said . . ." I started and Willy put his hand on my arm and shook his head.

"We'll skate tomorrow," Carl repeated. "It would be wrong now. It's too soft."

Stan turned back to his hoses, not mad, just ready to have Carl take over. It was like an old dog and a young dog where the old dog just shoulders up and the young one moves away without any fight.

We stood there for a while. There was something in Carl's voice that made it clear that nobody would be skating until the next day, even

31

if we wanted to, so we stood and looked at the new-blue of the ice on the rinks and while we were watching it that way Carl moved onto the left rink.

He didn't have skates on or anything, just street shoes with the laces sort of loose and the heels round and you would have thought he would have fallen on the ice but he didn't.

He walked around the rink carefully, just walked, taking short pulls from the bottle in his pocket, and when he'd gone all the way around, looking forward and down, he moved to the middle of the rink and raised his head and Willy whispered, "He's going to do it again. That strange thing."

But this time he didn't. He just stood with his head raised and said nothing and then he lowered his chin and turned and saw us staring at him and he smiled and walked past us into the warming house.

"Let's go in," Willy said. "I'm cold."

It wasn't cold, not as cold as it would get, but it was getting dark and there was light in the warming house so I nodded. It was as good an excuse as any to see more of Carl so I followed Willy in.

Inside the warming house it was all scars. Like the rink. Scars from skates and sticks and pocketknives. Carved initials and words in the wooden walls and the wooden benches that ran around the sides. Except for the ceiling no inch was bare, nothing was smooth but all rounded and worn and scarred. Dark round-soft wood.

In the middle of the room was a potbellied stove, black and worn, full of smoking birch with the flue open to make a small roar. The side glowed red, dull and hot. Overhead was one bulb, bare, with the hot wire showing inside.

Back to the rear was an army cot, steel, with a brown blanket that had a big US in the middle and a small pillow without a pillowcase, just stripes on a gray background.

And in the middle of the bunk sat Carl. There was nobody else in the warming house and he looked up when we came in, looked up and smiled with short yellow teeth. "Come in."

Willy nodded and went to the bench at the side near the stove and I followed still but couldn't think of a reason for doing it. I wasn't cold. I never got cold, except my heels in the hockey skates when it was deep cold in the middle of the hardest part of winter and we were playing and couldn't stop to go in and warm up.

But we sat down near the stove and Willy held his hands out as if he were warming them and I just sat and stared at the deep dull red on the side of the stove and wished I hadn't come in. I was working on a stick model at home, a model of a P-40 Warhawk and it was almost done, just the tissue left to glue on and I thought I should have been home doing that . . .

"You skaters?" Carl asked, cutting into my thinking, after we'd been sitting a long time.

Willy nodded. "All the time."

"Rinks will be open tomorrow."

"We heard you outside."

"Ahh." But he was just talking the way grownups usually talk to kids. Over and through while his mind worked on other things. It never failed when you were dealing with them—grownups talked like you weren't there. Except when they were chewing you out. Then they saw you.

Carl took another long pull from the bottle in his pocket and put it back and looked down for a moment and then up. He brushed something off his arm, looked at it, brushed it again and kept brushing it and I felt sad because I'd seen that before on Jimmy. Pisspot Jimmy had gone into deep problems with drinking, problems so he couldn't really walk or anything and they had to take him into that place for treatment and he was always brushing things off his legs. One time when I was just a kid and didn't know any better I asked him what he was brushing away and he told me it was bugs.

"I'm all over bugs," he'd said. "The little

monsters won't leave me alone." And of course there weren't any bugs at all, just in his head, and here Carl was brushing his arm the same way and any fool could see that he drank a lot so I just felt sad, the way you do when somebody has the bottle that way. But I was wrong.

"Either one of you got any saddle soap at home? This leather on the jacket is getting dried out, starting to crack bad. I should soap it down." He'd been rubbing the leather to smooth the cracks.

Willy stood up. "I've got some. I'll go get it."

"No. No. Just bring it tomorrow when you come to skate. That'll be fine." Another smile. "The jacket is my home. I should take care of it."

Which was a strange thing to say about his jacket, even if it was kind of true. Besides, the leather looked like it had never been cleaned and the bits of wool sticking through had surely never been rubbed with saddle soap or they'd be matted down more. It was dirty and grimy and the wool was gray to almost black but I didn't understand then that the jacket, and talking about the jacket, was the way Carl had when he drank.

We didn't know the jacket yet the way we would know it and understand it later when he talked about the plane.

"I'll bring the soap tomorrow," Willy promised. "For sure."

Since he was standing and I wanted to go pretty badly I stood up and went to the door and moved out into the cold where it was dark and Willy followed me for a change.

We walked with our breath out in front and I was thinking of Carl and I thought Willy was doing the same but after a bit he laughed.

"That Melonowski, he's something."

"Well, you can see why. Miss Johnson is really pretty."

"Sure. But right there in school like that. Huh. That takes something."

After that I went home and worked on the model Warhawk and did it fine except that I got some wrinkles in the tissue around the wing root and when I tried to wet them a little and take them out the paper got too wet and ruined it and I had to patch it with glue and more paper and of course that looked just awful.

My models always come out messy.

. : 5 : .

No matter how much you do in the summer, no matter how hard you work or run, your ankles always get weak. The muscles you use for skating don't get used in the summer and it's like everybody has to start all over in the fall, or the first part of winter when the ice forms and gets tight.

The next day was a Friday. School was school. But everybody brought skates and after school we hit the rinks and it was cold and dusky and we went into the warming house to put our skates on.

It was packed. It usually is the first few times after the ice is formed. But this time for some reason there were a lot of little kids, three and four, and like always they were having a rough time.

After skating gets going the warming house isn't so crowded. People skate and come in for a little, then back out, and cycle through that way. But when it first opens they just pack in and the little kids get pushed sideways until they're all in one corner, standing holding their skates, pouting and some of them starting to cry and always before they just had to fight it out or wait until the bigger kids were done and out skating.

But now there was Carl.

He was in the back of the shack and he stood up and he moved into the middle and he took a little girl by the hand and shouldered people out of the way and moved to the benches by the door. There were other kids sitting there, high-school kids suiting up for hockey and he looked at them.

That's all he did. Just looked at them, standing up with his flight jacket unzipped and the little girl holding onto his hand and Willy and I were sitting where we could see his eyes.

"They look hot," he said to me, leaning close to my ear. "His eyes look hot."

And they did. They almost glowed when he looked down at the kids who were sitting on the bench.

For a second or two they didn't do anything, and I think maybe they didn't want to do anything either. But the eyes cut through them, and they moved sideways and some of them got up and they left a place for the little girl and still Carl stood, looking down.

They moved more, made a wider place, and then the people in the center of the room parted and Carl raised his hand and the children who had been pushed down and down came through and they started to use the bench by the door and from that time on whenever the little kids came in they used that part of the bench and nobody else would use that place. Not even the grownups who came to skate to the music.

But it was Carl with the little girl that made me stare. With Willy it was the way he used his eyes to clear a spot for the little kids. But Willy sees things and I see lines, outsides of things, and Carl and the girl, the little girl, was all curving lines.

She was all in white with little white skates with colored pom-poms on the laces and she was three or maybe four and he leaned down and took her under the armpits and sat her on the bench.

Then his hands, hard and red and old and bent, took up the skates and untied the laces and helped her take off her boots and put the skates on, pulling them up soft and then hovering over the laces and tightening them for her, one at a time, all the time the curve of him looking down

39

at the skates. He looked like a great bird, his brown coat hanging open, the arms like wings coming down to pull the laces tight, then snug, and then helping her up and another child sat down and Carl's hands went down to the skates and worked magic, pulling them on and tightening them.

That's what I saw.

Willy saw inside of what was happening, saw something Carl was doing with the people inside and I saw the lines of what was happening; saw him bending over and down to help the little kids and I almost forgot to skate and maybe would have just sat and watched Carl but Willy nudged me.

"We've got to get out on the rink. Get our ankles started back." He clumped up and went for the door walking on his skate toes and I followed, staying up on the toes because they were sharp, new sharp, and there was some gravel on the road between the warming house and the rinks. Nothing dulls the skate blades like gravel.

We went right onto the hockey rink and just started skating around to the right. I left my stick at the gate because I didn't think I'd need it because they didn't have the nets out yet anyway.

My ankles felt like rubber but I could feel them

stiffening and pretty soon I was skating fast and I came up in back of Willy and threw a small body check at him, just playful, and he went down and got up and came back at me with one and I knew winter was going to be all right.

It was Friday and the ice was hard and the skates grabbed right with the new edges and starting Saturday we would get into hockey.

I forgot summer and fall the way you forget winter when it's summer or fall, just let it fall away and went to skating backwards and doing slow rolls dodging in and out of the other kids until it was stone dark and the lights came on and then we skated until our ankles screamed and went home to sleep hard and down thinking only of the ice and the cold.

. : 6 : .

It was during hockey that we first truly came to see how powerful Carl really was, saw how it came out and out of him, made people do what he needed them to do. We'd seen a bit of it that first night when he cleared the bench for the young kids—but during hockey we saw what it could really do.

Hockey at the McKinley rink had to be the closest you could come to war without killing somebody—a friendly war.

It wasn't hockey with rules, it wasn't hockey with a limited number of players, it wasn't hockey that ended or even began.

It was just hockey.

Nobody kept score, nobody chose up sides, nobody said who could play or who couldn't play.

ing, nothing compared to some of the shots we get.

Maybe it would be right to call it wild hockey, the way it would be played if there just weren't any rules and it was being played by jack-pine savages just out of the woods or something.

It started when you hit the ice and it ended when you went home and you played all the time. All winter. And there were no rules except that you couldn't intentionally use your stick to hook a guy in the gourds because one time Jimmy Nelson got hooked so bad he skated in little circles puking and it froze on the ice and we had to skate through that puke all winter.

Other than that no rules. Little kids skated on the left rink with the grownups until they thought they were ready for hockey and then they came onto the hockey rink. If they didn't make it they went back until they could handle it and that's how it went. Anybody could play hockey. Girls, boys, young, old—we even had some grownups on the hockey side now and then and they learned right away that when they hit the ice and got the puck they were no better and no worse than anybody.

Hot and wild and fast, twelve and fourteen hours a day of hockey on the weekends. If you got hurt you went to the warming house until the pain went down. If something broke they

In the right-hand rink hockey just went on and on, as long as the rink was open, all winter long; just the flash of skates and the shouts and swearing of kids as they slammed into the boards, the flat-*whap* of slap shots and the moans when somebody went down with a bad hit.

Hockey.

One time a kid came down from Canada and he played on a team up there, a high-school team, and he was good. He played left wing and he was really fast and he came to the rinks one day and when he got done he told me he'd never seen anything like it.

"That's the hardest hockey I've ever played," he said, sucking the blood out of a knuckle where a puck had smashed him. We didn't wear gloves. "Some of those small guys will kill you for the puck. Just kill you, eh?"

Naturally we'd played a little hard because we all knew he was from Canada and wanted to make a good impression. I threw a check into him once so hard he sprayed snot all over the ice and even if he was four years older I can hit pretty hard if I'm up to steam.

But even so, when you get a kid from Canada saying we play rough hockey you get an idea how the game goes. Merv Billings' mother wouldn't let him play with us anymore because he got a cracked rib and when he got that it was called your parents and you were out for the winter.

But the hockey went on. Pounding, slashing, cutting back and forth—the hockey went on. Sometimes there might be ten or twelve players on each side, between twenty and thirty players on the ice at the same time. With that many after the puck you felt lucky to see the thing, let alone get a shot, and if you actually got possession of it and tried to make a goal you could find yourself in the middle of an awful fight.

Hockey.

Blue and fast and tight. Sometimes you forgot how cold it was and your feet would freeze until your heels felt like lumps and you had to go in and sit through hot pain until they thawed and then back out into the fight. There was crying and there was screaming and there was speed and there was movement so fast and wild that you could forget who you were, forget everything but the ice and the speed and the game that went on and on and didn't start and didn't end.

But now and then things could go wrong. Not often, but sometimes, and when they did there was usually a fight to get things squared away and if there wasn't a fight there would be cutting—somebody who was bad, really bad, would be cut out of the game and not allowed to play.

That's how we came to see what Carl could do—when Dalen Erickson got cut.

It came fast. He high-sticked a little kid in the face and that wasn't so bad if it happened by accident. The kid bled a little and it stopped and he went back into the game and that should have been the end of that. But Dalen did it again, and I saw him, and he smiled when he did it—hooked the kid hard on purpose and there was more blood this time and I skated up to Willy.

"That Dalen, he hooked the little kid on purpose."

"Yeah. I saw it."

"Just to see the kid bleed."

"Yeah."

"So we've got to do something about it."

Willy looked at me, then back to Erickson who was skating around the rear of the net. Erickson was big. Really big. "He's a junior in high school," Willy said, looking at me again. "He'll kill us. We're just going into the eighth grade. He'll really kill us. I don't want to die."

But he knew we had to do something just as I knew it. When somebody acts mean that way you just have to do something about it. If you don't it just comes back later. Once on my paper route I had a big kid take my money and I gave it to him because he said he'd leave me alone and naturally he was lying. He kept coming back and finally I had to fight him, which I did and used a brick to make up for size and hit him so hard he goobered like a sick cat and went down. The point was that I might as well have fought him in the first place and saved the money.

Still. I didn't want to die either. "Why don't we talk to him?" I looked down at the ice. "Maybe we could just explain it . . ."

But it never came up. The little kid ran for the warming house and went inside and pretty soon Carl came out.

He wasn't running, but he walked kind of quick and the little kid was with him and he pointed out Erickson on the ice and Carl made a sign with his hand for Erickson to come off the ice.

Erickson ignored it and tried to go back to playing but by now we'd all stopped and were just standing, looking at Erickson and Carl.

Carl made another sign and Erickson still ignored him. The big kid skated to the other end of the rink and shook his head and just kept skating back and forth.

Carl set the little kid aside and opened the rink gate and walked out on the ice. He didn't look mad, but more sad, and he walked to the center of the rink and stood. No more signs, he just stood and looked at Erickson and we could all see the power come out of him and go across the ice and Willy swore under his breath and saw inside of what was happening but I saw the lines again.

Carl standing straight and clean and tall and his eyes locked onto Erickson, a straight line across the ice.

And Erickson skating back and forth, fighting the eyes the way a northern pike fights the hook, tearing back and forth and skating around the rink, wilder and faster and faster with all of us standing and watching until finally he could stand it no more, until none of us could stand it any longer and he skate-ran to the gate and off the ice and into the warming house.

We still stood, staring.

Carl moved his eyes around the rink, from one face to the next, then he made a signal to the small kid and the kid came on the ice and Carl ruffled his cap so it came down over his eyes.

Then he did another strange thing. He picked up the kid, held him out in front of him at arm's length and went around in a circle slowly, almost as if he were offering the kid to us, then around again a little faster and swooping the kid up and down.

And without skates, on the ice, never losing his balance, and finally around one more time to set the kid down, gently—and then he turned and walked off the ice and into the warming house.

That's when I thought of the dancing part. The lines all went around and swooped down and out and the kid's skates flashed out in a silver circle, around the rink, and the line curved down so the kid came down to the ice and I thought of a troop of dancers who had come to the school one time.

They were modern dancers and they said how the dances were supposed to mean something but they weren't as good as Carl. Or maybe they were as good but they didn't mean it as much. Or maybe Carl wasn't dancing but just being and they didn't know how to do that.

Whatever it was, when Carl went down and out and around with the kid I thought of dancing and in my head I called him Dancing Carl and later when I told Willy that was what I'd named him Willy agreed. Except that he wanted to find the reason that Carl danced because he always looked inside things and I just wanted to see him do it again. I didn't care so much why he did it, just that he did it.

But none of that helped Erickson. He was cut, cut away and gone and we saw him leave the warming house later and he didn't skate all the rest of the winter. And Carl never said a word.

He just used his eyes and something else we didn't understand, something that came from inside him, something that was from a sadness we couldn't understand but so strong that when it came out nothing could stop it. His eyes stopped Erickson, drove him off the rink; his eyes and the strong thing that came out of him.

. : 7 : .

Willy always says that there are really two
worlds, not one. He says that there is a grownup
world and there is a world for us and he likes
ours a lot better. I don't know for sure about all
of that but when it came to Carl there were at
first two ways to see him, our way and the
grownup way. And even though they both came
together and there was just the one Carl, just
the one Dancing Carl, it's not fair to show just
one side.

We saw him at the rinks as having the power
to make things happen, saw him making the
lines go out and out of him, saw him as part of
the ice, part of the warming house, controlling
it all.

The grownups I think at first saw him as the

town drunk and they were just helping out by giving him the job at the rinks and a place to sleep and maybe that was true. At first.

But it changed. It changed for the grownups as much as it did for all of us and Willy and I first saw the change coming down in the back of Severson's Bakery before daylight one morning.

Severson had run the bakery ever since he took over from his father, who had run the bakery when he took it over from *his* father. There'd always been a Severson's Bakery and sometimes we would go to school early just so we could stop at Severson's and go in the back.

They started baking the day's bread and rolls and pastry about three in the morning and by eight on a winter morning the smells that came out of the bakery made your mouth wet and your stomach rumble.

We would go in the back, out of the dark cold of the morning with our hair frozen and our fingers stiff and just stand inside the door and let the smells work into us. Hot smells of fresh bread and rolls, just coming out of the big rotating ovens and when the bakers—there were three of them—when the bakers saw us standing there they would snake a couple of rolls off the racks, fresh and so hot you couldn't hold them, and throw them to us.

It's hard to think of anything better. Just coming out of the cold into the smell of the bread and eating hot rolls while the steam and heat works around you—Willy says it's a memory that will stay with us the rest of our lives but I think we should keep going back to make sure. Go back a lot.

One morning after Carl had been at the rinks for a couple of weeks, after the business with Dalen, we stopped at the bakery and they gave us a roll and then the cooks started talking while we were eating them.

They were talking about Carl, talking while they worked, sliding the big pans into the ovens, and Bud, who is the master baker, smiled.

"You hear about that crazy Wenstrom down at the rinks?"

The other two cooks didn't say anything. He always had young cooks there and they would study with him for a while and then move on and they never talked much because Bud did most of the talking.

"I guess he's been doing some pretty weird stuff. Dancing or moving or something. And he's taken over the rinks like it was his town or something . . ."

Still the two other cooks didn't speak but Willy and I were listening carefully now. We knew the other side of Carl.

Bud had been sliding a pan into the big oven

and he stopped and thought, then pushed it in. "I was skating there the other night, two nights ago, and Carl was there and he didn't seem weird or anything. He just seemed, well, like Carl—like he's been since the war. Since he came back. Of course I was only there for a couple of hours but there are some who say they've seen it and it's kind of pretty. Like maybe he's got the shine on him or something. But I don't know, I don't know—maybe we should skate a little more and see what it's like . . ."

And that was the end of it because he started to talk about a girl he'd met in the army once, down south someplace, and just when the story started to get good Willy pulled at my arm and we had to go to make school. Willy said he'd heard the story before but I didn't believe him because when I asked him how it ended he wouldn't tell me. Kept saying I was too young and that it wasn't a true story anyway because he'd heard his cousin who is in the navy tell it about a girl in California. I said it didn't matter if a story was true or not as long as it was a good story and we argued the rest of the way to school about that one.

But later I heard other grownups talking and they felt about like Bud, felt like maybe Carl was strange but that there was more, too. More that they had to watch.

. : 8 : .

There was music at the rinks.

From the hockey side you almost couldn't hear it because the speakers were hung up in the wire and in the trees and all aimed at the left rink for the grownups who liked to skate to the music. Besides, there was usually so much noise on the hockey side you couldn't hear it anyway.

But there was music there, from a record player that was kept under Carl's bunk. It was one of those old military record players, probably from the war, and it played scratchy and wobbly but they had a selection of waltzes and polkas and Carl would put records on when he opened the rinks after school and play a whole stack that night. The music didn't make any sense at first, he would just play them the way they came, but it was always in the background.

Loud and scratching in the cold and after the dark came down and the lights came on the music matched the rink lights somehow. It would come dim, but then louder and seemed to be flat and moving at the same time—just like the small bulbs made the rinks all flat light, the music spilled out of the speakers and over the cold ice.

We almost never skated to the music except one time when Shirley came down to the rinks and I got brave and asked her to skate. That took something, that did. She had her hair in a pony tail and a stocking cap on so it framed her face and her eyes kind of lifted at the corners and I thought I would die, my knees hurt so bad.

But Willy dared me and it was the kind of dare you couldn't really put away so I stuck my stick in the snow at the end of the rink and went out of the hockey rink and over onto the other side where she was skating. I caught her halfway around the rink and kind of moved in beside her smooth and easy and swallowed hard and said, "Would you like to skate with me?"

I think. Actually I don't remember what I said but I know she nodded, I saw her nod and I took her hand and we skated around the rink four times.

Of course Willy made a thing of it and teased me when I skated past him but he was just jealous and I knew it and kept skating. After four rounds to the music she said she had to go and I nodded and let go her hand. I was pretty near crushing it anyway. And I thought it was just an excuse but it wasn't. She really went into the warming house and took her skates off and went home and that made me feel some good. Except that I couldn't remember a thing that I said or that she said and I sat for hours that night until I fell asleep and still couldn't remember.

We sat and talked a lot. Willy was great for talking and even though I didn't start that way some of Willy had a way of rubbing off on you like I guess some of me rubbed off on Willy.

Like during study period we would try to get in the back and talk, or whisper. Or maybe pass notes if Melon was running the study period because he'd crack you for talking and when he cracked you it would sometimes turn blue.

After that time with Erickson and how he got cut from the rink we talked about Carl. In fact for the rest of that winter we talked about Carl. Even now, when it's all done, we still talk about Carl and I think maybe the whole town still talks about Carl.

"How could that be?" Willy whispered at me in study period.

"What?" I had a watchful eye on Melon but he was staring at the wall next to the window.

Or maybe out the window. Or thinking of Miss Johnson.

"How could it be, what Carl did?" Willy made a frown. "Down at the rink. With Erickson."

I didn't know. "Maybe we're not supposed to know where that power comes from. Maybe that's just for certain grownups."

"Drunks?"

"He's not a drunk."

"He is too."

"No he's not." And this time it came out almost too loud. Melon looked up and covered the room with his eyes and I waited with my breath held but it passed and he went back to staring at the wall. "I don't know what he is but he's not a drunk. Pisspot Jimmy is a drunk, not Carl."

Pisspot Jimmy lived down in back of the Mint Cafe in some boxes and he was always wet with himself and that's how he got his name. But he could never remember anything or even walk or talk and was just considered dead or gone. He could never do what Carl did, could never be what we'd seen Carl be.

"Maybe Carl is a drunk," I whispered, "because he drinks all the time. But there's more, too."

Wham! I took a shot down on my head, a straight-down knuckle shot that crossed my eyes. Old Melon had gone around and caught me from the rear and just about put my lights out.

"Quit talking," he said quietly. *"Now."*

"Yes sir."

"Next time I'll pop you hard."

"Yes sir." I closed my eyes and tried to figure if the colors I saw were normal or from his knuckle. They faded slowly. Knuckle colors.

"You talk too loud," Willy whispered as soon as Melon was gone. "Hold it down."

"Let's not talk at all."

"I want to know more about Carl."

"So wait until we get to the rinks."

Which was what we did and was why we got more involved in what Carl's dances meant than other people in town. Or more involved in Carl.

But there was one more thing that happened before Willy got inside Carl and I saw more than lines with Carl's dancing.

Finding out about Carl is one of those back-door things. We kept doing things that didn't seem to have anything to do with Carl only to find that they all mattered later. Like finding out about Melon and Miss Johnson and it didn't seem to have anything to do with Carl except that it showed us what we thought might be love only to find that what Carl danced later to Helen Swanson was different and maybe real love.

And we started to get inside of Carl because David Hanson made a crack about my P-40 Warhawk.

. : 9 : .

It wasn't that David was mean. He isn't. He's the next-door neighbor on one side of my house and there isn't one on the other side because we live on the edge of town.

And you'd think that living right next to each other we'd be good friends but that just didn't happen. He's a year older than me and his folks are kind of churchy and mine aren't and we just do different things.

But David came over one day after school and saw my Warhawk model after I'd painted it.

"You could have masked it," he said. "And not had those fuzzy edges around the paint."

And it was a little fuzzy around the tiger mouth, but not bad, but it bothered me. I thought it meant something that I had a messy model and his were always neat and that both-

ered me and I set out to make a model that was
neat and real looking and hard to do and then
when he came over he wouldn't be able to say
anything.

I got a stick model B-17—a big, four-engined
bomber from the Second World War—and I
worked four nights almost all through the night
until it was finished and there were no wrinkles
and the paint lines were clean and sharp and I
hung it from the ceiling in my room. Naturally
David didn't come over to see it, because that's
the way those things seem to work.

But it turned out to have a lot to do with Carl,
maybe some of it good and maybe some of it not
so good.

It got us inside what Carl was and like I said
it was a backdoor kind of thing.

What happened to bring things all into one
place and make Carl more than he'd been before
was that a kid named Billy Krieg took sick and
went down and down with it and they got him
into the hospital but everybody said he was
going to die.

So they had a big skating party to raise money
for some special operation that Billy was supposed to have and it all would have been pretty
nice.

They got some new records and put a new

needle in the phonograph and opened both rinks for the party so there wasn't any hockey that night. It was a Tuesday night so they started the skating party early and everybody had to pay a dollar to get in and a quarter a dance, only it wasn't dancing of course but just skating to the music with your favorite girl. I only had to pay fifty cents, being twelve, and I had three quarters besides and you can guess who I spent them on and we skated together after my quarters were gone too and it didn't matter if Willy teased me some.

But Willy found a girl too—David's sister Sharon Hanson—and we skated on the hockey side and it was like being a soldier taking your girl on the battlefield after the war is over, skating on the hockey side of the rinks with a girl holding your arm and talking about the night and the music and the school and everything like that.

It would have been nice except that during the night while we were all skating around and being happy Billy Krieg died in the hospital and I saw the sheriff come and whisper something to some of the grownups at the end of the rink.

In a few minutes it went around the rinks, like a fire; we all knew that Billy had died and we all felt sad but the music kept going and some of us kept skating because we were moving when we heard it and on skates you just keep on moving.

It was like something had stopped but had to keep going, too, and the music that was supposed to have meant something happy suddenly meant something sad but it still worked.

I saw people skating and crying while the music played and they went around and around and I guess maybe I was crying too. Because I had known Billy too and he was all right, but more than that it was the sadness of the night and what had happened—more than who it happened to.

I cried and skated around and Shirley on my arm cried and everybody just kept going around and then Carl came on the ice.

He didn't have skates on but he walked out in the middle of the ice and as I skated by I could see tears in his eyes but that might have been from the cold or the bottle in his pocket because there were often tears in his eyes, and he danced.

This time it wasn't just a movement or a turn. He danced with his arms out to the side, around and around with his hands making those swooping motions and he moved back and forth with the top of his body as his arms swept and it came from the music and it didn't come from the music, too.

He grew out of the ice. Everybody stopped

skating and watched him and he grew out of the ice in curving lines and I stood with Shirley and we watched Carl go around and back and forth with his feet, his shoes, sliding on the frayed ice, torn from the blades to make a film of scraping.

He danced and grew and moved around the rink not once but twice, twice around in great swoops of beauty out of the ice and then he was gone back into the warming house and still nobody moved and I thought of Billy Krieg.

In just that way I stood still and something from the dance or of the dance or the way Carl had grown from the ice in swoops and curves made me think of Billy Krieg and it wasn't sad. I thought of how I had known him before he was sick.

A clean thought about Billy.

And then everybody started skating again. Not suddenly, all at once, but one and two and three and pretty soon all moving to the music and Willy came up to me.

Sharon was gone—she'd left with her parents—and Willy got on the other side of Shirley.

"You ever seen anything like that?" He was smiling but it was painted on. "I mean wasn't that something?"

Shirley nodded. I didn't say anything.

"I want to talk to him," Willy said. "I want to talk to him now."

And he skated for the warming house, through all the skaters and I took Shirley's hand hard and started to follow but Shirley pulled loose. "I don't want to talk just now. I'll skate for a while."

And I was caught between but I wanted to see what it was with Carl and I nodded and left her there and went to the warming house with Willy.

. : 10 : .

He was sitting on his bunk, at the end opposite the pillow, just sitting staring at the stove, which had a red-gray glow on the side.

Carl looked tired—no, more than that, he looked smaller. Like he'd carved part of himself off to do the dance on the ice and his eyes were glazed over and in a funny way he was alone. There were other people in the warming house, of course, but Carl was alone on his bunk staring at the stove and people made an effort not to see him, as if he might be embarrassed if they looked at him.

Willy sat on the bench next to his bunk and I stood for a minute, then sat.

We didn't say anything and I thought maybe we should get up and go outside again because Carl didn't even notice that we were there.

His eyes went through the stove, into the red glow and through and Willy coughed. "That was really something, the way you moved out there on the ice."

Carl said nothing.

"Did you learn that somewhere? How to move like that so people would think of things?"

Carl turned from the stove then and his eyes went to Willy, then through Willy. It was as if Willy weren't there.

He coughed, took the bottle from his pocket and took a sip to make the cough go away. Two swallows, then three, then another short cough and the bottle went back into the pocket.

"Was it like a school?" Willy insisted. He was ever one for sticking to a thing, chewing it until it was nothing but a frazzle. I stood up because I was pretty sure Carl wasn't going to talk to us. But I was wrong.

"School?" Carl asked, bringing his eyes back to Willy's face. It wasn't that he was drunk, or maybe he was but it didn't affect him that much. It was more that he was still out on the ice, or somewhere else. "What about school?"

"Did you learn to dance like that at a school?"

"What dance?"

"Out there, on the ice. The dance you did— that was neat. Did you learn it at a school?"

Carl looked at him for a long time, studying his face closely. Then he smiled. "You're young.

You're just a boy. It's all movement—not a dance. Everything in life is a movement, a swirl, a spin. And the movements have color. Like some swirls are red and some are green and some are blue like the ice and they all mix together and everything in life is a movement of color to music."

And of course I thought he was crazy. But Willy nodded and smiled. It was like he understood something and I thought maybe Willy was crazy, too, and then I remembered that I saw everything in lines and maybe Carl wasn't crazy. Or maybe we were all crazy.

"You're nodding but you don't see it," Carl said, looking into Willy's eyes now, straight in and down. "Nothing in life is without movement and the movement has color and I see the movement and the colors all the time. Sometimes it's nice and sometimes it hurts . . ."

And that's as much as he said, even though Willy tried to get him to talk more about it. He went back to staring at the stove, ignoring us and the people who came and went in the warming house and we went back outside to skate.

I found Shirley but she was skating with Phil Barret who is a year older and good at football which I don't play so that took care of that. It was probably just as well because if I'd have gotten serious about Shirley I wouldn't have learned about Carl later. But at the time it stung a little.

We moved around the rink and everybody was still skating sad and after a time I went back in and took my skates off and walked home and left Willy at the rinks.

Once on the way home I tried to move around in swirls and think of colors and something that made it all happen but nothing came out right. I didn't even see lines, so I stopped. It wasn't the kind of thing you wanted to be caught doing walking down a dark street in your own neighborhood.

I was just at my door when it hit me that nobody thought Carl was strange for doing it. Here he had gone and twirled around without skates on and the whole rink had stopped to watch him and nobody had said a word or thought it was out of place. If I were seen doing it I would probably be locked up.

But when Carl did it, it was like something that was supposed to happen. And then I remembered that his dance had made me think about Billy Krieg, something in the dance had made me think about Billy, and that kept me up half the night thinking about it.

. : II : .

There were these rumors about Carl, things they said at school or around town or down at Crazy Joe's Bar.

He was an ex-convict who killed someone and lived with it on his head and drank to hide it.

He had stolen a lot of money and hidden it and a woman had stolen it and he drank to hide it.

He once had a wife and she took all his money and ran off with the man who delivered propane gas and was living somewhere in Montana.

He had a bunch of children he'd deserted and he couldn't stand the shame of it and had to drink.

He had once danced with a great ballet company somewhere in Europe but took to drink and it destroyed him.

He was actually only twenty-eight years old and the drink had burned him out and left him looking old.

His family had been burned in a house fire and he had started it by smoking in bed and the memory of it drove him into the bottle.

He had been driven out of a town somewhere in Kansas for doing something they wouldn't even talk about but for which they would hang him if he ever came back.

He had fought in the Second World War and done something wrong and couldn't live with the memory.

All of these things were said about him and maybe some of them were true and maybe they weren't true but nobody could say for sure because the people who said those things never once asked him about what he had or had not done. They just talked.

Nobody except Willy and when Willy asked him it broke Carl, broke him like a motor inside had stopped. Or maybe it was my fault. I should maybe have known better than to bring the B-17 to the rinks.

But whoever did it or didn't do it, Carl was broken and I think would have died or stayed down and broken if it hadn't been for Helen and Carl falling in love. That brought him up, brought the whole town up, but I think for a little time there he was awfully close to dying.

. : 12 : .

It started on a Thursday afternoon when we went down to the rinks even though they were closed. There were some powerful winds blowing and snow and cold and most people didn't go out but Willy came over and had his skates with him and said something about going skating and I thought why not.

Which was my first mistake. The second one was that I took the B-17 with me. That's not as crazy as it sounds. Somebody in school had mentioned the fact that Carl might have been a pilot on a B-17 during the war and I was kind of proud of the model and I thought he might like to see it even if David Hanson hadn't come to look at it.

School was closed due to the weather, something that didn't happen that often in McKinley, and I thought the way it was blowing we'd probably spend most of our time in the warming house anyway. The wind chill must have been seventy or eighty below and for anybody who hasn't walked five blocks in heavy wind and cold carrying a stick model of a B-17 and a pair of hockey skates and a hockey stick I can tell you not to bother. I probably won't be doing it again soon.

Willy of course thought I was nuts but I'd spent a lot of time on that model and if Carl had actually flown in a B-17 I didn't want to miss a chance to talk to him about it.

Somehow we got to the rinks, either with the B-17 flying and carrying me along or with me holding it down, and there wasn't anybody skating.

Not even any kids. So we went in the warming house half figuring it would be closed but Carl was sitting on his bunk.

He smiled when we came in, then his face tightened in a quick frown when he saw the plane but I didn't think anything of it.

We knocked snow off and I put the skates and stick in a corner. There was nobody else in the warming house either.

"What's that?" he said, pointing at the stick model.

"It's a model I made. It's a B-17."

"I know that. I know what it is. I mean why do you have it here at the rink?"

"I told him he was crazy . . ." Willy started, laughing.

"Get it out of here."

His voice was quiet, almost like a still pond. Not mad sounding or sad, maybe a little afraid, but so quiet and still that I couldn't quite hear it.

"What?"

"Please take it outside. The model. Please take it out now."

"But it's just a model. If I take it out the wind will tear it apart." Like I said, I had a lot of work in it. I'd probably ruin it later, the way you do with models. Maybe put lighter fluid on the tail and send her off a roof. But that was later, now it was still a fresh model and I hated to just throw it out in the snow and let the wind tear it apart. "I'll put it over in the corner."

"Did you have something to do with B-17's during the war?" Willy asked and it was something he shouldn't have asked, not then, not ever.

Carl turned from the plane to Willy and there was a hunted look in his eyes. No, more than that, more a torn thing, a broken thing—as if something inside had ripped and torn loose and left him broken and he looked at the model and his face wrinkled down and I knew it wasn't a model anymore, knew he wasn't in the warming house.

"Colors," he said, whispering. "Colors red and down and going around and around in tighter and tighter circles. Hot. Colors hot and alive and going down."

Willy stepped back. "I'm sorry. I didn't mean to say anything . . ."

But it was done. His whisper changed to a hiss, hot and alive, and he stood in the warming house and got into the open place by the door. I dumped the model in a corner, dumped it without looking, and moved away.

Carl stood with his arms out, still making that hissing sound, and I wondered if I could get out of the warming house and go for help, get the police, but he was by the door and I was afraid to go past him. Not afraid that he'd do something to me, afraid that I'd hurt him somehow.

So I stood, we stood, and Carl moved his arms even tighter out and the hiss changed to a kind of growl and I realized that he was a plane, a large plane, and I could see it wheeling through the sky, engines rumbling and I knew then that it was a B-17.

Through two, then three loops around the open area in the warming house Carl moved, turning and banking slowly and I swear you could see the plane.

Then something happened. Something hit or

hurt the plane, one arm, one wing folded up and over and the plane went down, circling in a great spiral as it went down.

I mean Carl. Carl went down. But it was a plane, too. There in the warming house there was something that Carl did that made him seem a great bomber with a broken wing going down, around and down and I could see it. See the smoke and the explosion as the shell took the wing, the way I'd seen it in newsreels, and then the plane coming down, all the lines coming down, down to the ground in a crash that was like a plane and like a bird, too.

Down and down and crashing into the ground and Carl lay on the floor by the stove and I couldn't see him breathing and I leaned down. Willy came from the back of the room.

But he wasn't dead. Not yet. He couldn't move and he smelled and I leaned down to take his arm and Willy took the other one.

"He stinks," I said. "What's that smell?"

"He went in his pants."

"God."

"Let's get him on the bunk."

We horsed and pulled until finally he was on the bunk. Or at least the top half was up on the bunk. Then we jacked around until we got his legs up.

"I think we should get a doctor or something," I said, looking down at him. "He doesn't look so good."

His face was gray, gray to white, and there was some of the gummy stuff in the corners of his mouth that I saw on Uncle Raymond when he died of a stroke. But Willy took my hand and pulled me away from the bunk. "I don't know what good it would do, and besides, I don't think we should leave him."

"But what can we do?"

"I don't know. But I don't think it's good to leave him right now. He might need us."

To be with him when he dies, I thought. That's all that came through. And I knew it was wrong, but I thought maybe Willy was right—we should be with him. I moved away from the door and Carl suddenly sat up.

He turned and put his feet on the floor and his face down in his hands and then took the bottle out of his pocket and drank long and hard. I thought he was all right, was over it, but he wasn't. He'd just moved into the next part.

He stared past us, or maybe that isn't quite right either. He didn't stare so much as just not look at anything—when I looked at his eyes I thought that he wasn't there, was somewhere else.

"We were ten and now there is only one," he said, his voice flat, toneless.

When he said nothing further Willy leaned forward. "It's all right, Carl. It's all right."

"No. It isn't. We were ten and now we are only one and she is gone." He was crying now and I felt awful because he was hurt, hurt deep and I thought maybe somehow we had done it. "She is gone, curling down in fire and heat and gone to hell with all of them and I'm the only one alive."

He stopped and kind of weaved and I thought he was either going to pass out or fall back on the bunk but he kept on.

"We were going to Bremen and there were ten of us and she was the Lucky Doll, the Lucky Lady who never let us down but we took one in the wing root and she crumpled, crumpled and started down and the fire started up, started as we whipped around in the tight spin the tight spin the tight spin . . ."

He stopped for breath then, took it deep and hard, then talked again, his words tight and fast, slamming one against the next so hard they almost ran over each other.

". . . oh God the tight spin and the fire came then all red and roaring and hot and then the explosion and I was blown clear. Only me. I was clear and falling next to the Lucky Doll, falling with her falling around and around down towards the ground with the burning Lady, dancing with the burning Lady to the ground while the fire took her and I was the only one, the only one left . . ."

Another breath and again we thought he was done and Willy said: "It's all right. It's all right," the way he had done when Barbara Tilson's puppy was hit by the grain truck except then it wasn't all right because the puppy was dying and it wasn't all right now because I was sure Carl was dying.

"No!" He screamed it. "NO. NO. It wasn't all right because I danced with her, danced with the Lucky Doll down and down and when I looked to her I saw Jimmy in the belly turret, saw Jimmy in the belly turret and he was looking right at me and his legs, his legs were on fire and he was in the Lucky Doll and I was out and free and he was burning and he looked right at me, dancing down and down and then he tried to choke himself with his microphone cord, choke himself and I wanted to help him, down and down I danced with the Lucky Doll, danced with the lady with the hole in her stocking and her knees keep a knocking dance to the light of the moon . . ."

He sang the last in a kind of Oriental singsong voice, sang it high and low, and then fell over on the bunk and I thought he was gone.

Willy leaned over. "He's still breathing. Help me with his legs."

We got his legs up on the bunk again and this

time he didn't come to but stayed asleep, or passed out and we sat back on the benches.

"We've done a terrible thing," I said, looking down at Carl. "Without meaning to we've done some kind of a terrible thing."

Willy looked at him, lying in the smell, and he shook his head. "No. Not us. Somebody did, somebody back then did a terrible thing to him but it wasn't us. We just reminded him of it."

We sat in the shack for hours after that, talking about Carl and how it must have been to dance with a falling B-17 or see your friend burn and finally, when it got late and he was still out cold, afraid to stay and afraid to go, we left and walked home.

We banked the stove before we left, loaded it with birch and turned the damper down, so Carl wouldn't freeze to death and then we left him there, with the stove cooking and the light on.

I was sure that when we came back he would either be dead or gone and I knew I wasn't going to sleep. Halfway home I threw the model in a garbage can, threw the work away, and maybe I cried some and I thought how awful it was that you could mean well and do so much damage to somebody. I really thought then that Carl was broken, a broken thing and we had done the breaking and Willy agreed and we didn't see any hope for Carl, for what we had done.

But that was before Helen came.

$\cdot$: 13 : $\cdot$

Sometimes things mix. Sometimes you seem to start with something that's by itself and you think it will stay that way but then it mixes and it's all different. Like when you mix two colors of paint in art class and you get something completely new and different.

Part of the rinks that winter with Carl is like that. It started with hockey, with skating, just like it always did, and then it started to mix with the feelings of Billy Krieg dying and that mixed with the way we broke Carl without meaning to break him and finally Helen . . .

On the hockey side it was always like war, and when you were playing you didn't notice much. But for some strange reason we all knew the day Helen came. We all noticed.

Four days after Willy and I had broken Carl

we went back to the rinks. We went without knowing what to expect but Carl was still there only different. He just sat on the bunk, sat with his bottle but he didn't help the little kids with their skates and he didn't come out and study the rinks or dance or say anything.

He just sat.

But in the winter you skated and so Willy and I came back to the rinks and we put on our skates and went on the hockey rink but my heart wasn't in it. I took four or five good body shots that left me with a bloody nose and a swollen ear and I still couldn't get into the game and twice I saw Willy go down with solid checks and all I could think of was Carl. Finally we moved away from the play to the side of the boards next to the grownup rink and there was Helen.

She was skating to the music on the other side, or just skating around, and the reason I noticed her was because she made me think of those old paintings you see of people skating. The way the people at the rink normally skated they just looked regular, like they'd come off the street and put skates on and started going around.

But Helen looked different. She was an older woman with gray hair, but she was trim looking and had on small white skates and wore a wool or tweed skating suit with a fur collar. The suit was a little frayed at the edges but something about her, something about the way she held her head, made that not matter. Her skirt was kind of long, too, longer than other skirts but that didn't matter either. She had her hands stuck in a fur muff that matched her collar and on her head was one of those square little hats like they wear in Russia and it was of the same fur.

She looked like she'd just stepped out of one of those paintings you see on calendars or matchboxes and Willy and I stared at her while she skated around the rink.

Even her skating made you think of a painting. She skated straight up and down, really controlled, with short strokes of her blades that kept her moving but without bending.

"Who is she?" Willy asked. By now most of the skaters had stopped to look at her, most of the hockey players, and nobody knew her name.

Finally Eunice Moen, who was skating on the other side and had a crush on Willy but who Willy didn't like, skated over to the boards and nodded. "You watching Helen?" she asked.

"Is that her name?" I saw her take a turn and keep moving without seeming to move her skates. "Where did she come from?"

"Somebody said she just moved into town. I heard them call her Helen but I don't know her last name. Helen something." Eunice looked at Willy and smiled and Willy tried not to see her.

"She's sure something," he said, and I nodded and then I looked over at the door of the warming house which was opening, and Carl stepped out.

I poked Willy. "Look."

Carl was a little bent but he straightened and walked down to the rink and stood by the gate. He must have seen Helen in the warming house when she put on her skates, but he stood now and watched her as if seeing her for the first time. Two, three circuits of the rink she made while he watched and I knew then that he was coming out of it, coming out of our breaking him, and I smiled and thought that if it meant nothing it was still nice that just seeing this Helen was worth it to bring him out.

But there was more there, more than I saw. Helen continued to skate around the rink but Carl changed as he watched her. He didn't just straighten, he stood taller, and his body seemed to fill and his neck got tighter and his eyes were sharp as he watched and it was just like watching somebody being born.

On the fourth lap, as she went by, skating all up and down and proper, Carl's hand went up. It was a short movement, a small round movement; his fingers made a tight little circle but Willy saw it and so did I and Willy smiled.

At the other end of the rink Helen stopped and

leaned over to tighten her skate a little and while she was bent over away from the gate Carl came onto the ice.

He moved from the gate towards her, just a few steps, then he stopped and turned away. One short step back, his back arched, and now the whole rink was watching, everybody but Helen, who was still facing away and now he turned back.

Slowly his arms came up and he turned around, let his arms swoop down and up, then stopped, his hands out to his sides and his eyes locked onto Helen as she stood, finished tightening her skates, and turned to see the rink all stopped, watching Carl, watching her.

She saw Carl standing, his arms out, a small smile on his mouth, little puffs of steam coming from his mouth and nose.

She didn't see what we saw.

We saw Carl, who had been hurt but who now was coming back as king of the rinks, with his power back, with his dance back, with his eyes back. We saw Carl.

She saw an old drunk who was acting weird and she turned away from him, turned away from Carl and skated to the left in the circle to the music that was still playing and it broke something, broke maybe a spell and everybody went back to skating and I felt sad for Carl.

For him to come out of where he had been when we broke him, for him to change and come out and have it thrown in his face was awful and maybe I hated Helen for that a little.

But I was wrong again. About Carl. About Helen.

Carl was just starting.

.⋮ 14 ⋮.

"People think the only way to get anything done is by talking," Willy said to me once after the winter with Carl at the rinks was all over. "They have conferences and talk and talk—how wrong can you be?"

Willy always thought along those lines. It was part of trying to see inside of things. If somebody said there was a way to do a thing, Willy would just naturally sit down and try to find a different way. It wasn't hole-picking, it was more that he wanted to make sure there wasn't a better way to do something.

"Take Carl," he said, leaning back on the side of the Poplar River during the hot time of the afternoon when the fish didn't bite anyway. "Carl never said a word to Helen and look how that turned out."

"Yes," I said, nodding. "But that was Carl. And most people aren't like Carl."

And for a change Willy agreed with me.

"That's for sure," he said. "That's for darn sure. There's never been anything like Carl. Man, when he set his sights on Helen that was something to see—I almost forgot about hockey."

I heard one of the grownups say that Carl was courting Helen the old way, and maybe that's right. But I can't believe there were that many Carls running around in the old days. I think Carl was courting Helen in his own way, with his power.

And it was something to see.

Usually at the rinks Carl just stacked the records into the machine any old way. You might get a waltz next to a polka and a schottische next to some kind of military march but all that changed when Helen came down to the rinks.

And she did come back. The next night she came to skate and I was in the warming house when she arrived and she sat in the corner and put her skates down in little controlled movements that made tight small lines in my mind.

So straight she sat, in the corner, straight up and back and Carl got up off his bunk and came over to her and bowed. A short jerk of his head forward and down.

She looked up and then down, ignored him, but he kneeled in front of her anyway.

I turned for Willy but he had gone outside onto the rink and I was alone except for some high-school kids.

Carl's hands went down and they picked up Helen's white skates with white laces and the red pom-poms and he loosened the laces. Then he slipped off her fur-lined boots and pulled the skates on and the hard red hands tightened the laces, not too tight, not too loose—just snug.

She said nothing. He said nothing. Helen took it like maybe it was supposed to happen, that Carl was supposed to help her with her skates, and she tried not to look down at him but I saw her slip a couple of times and glance down while he was bent over pulling on the lace.

When her laces were tight he stood, uncoiled up and away from her and made all the curved lines straight and looked down and gave that same tight bow again. Just a movement of the chin, and went back to his bunk and sat on the edge with his back straight, the fur collar of his flight jacket up, his legs together. Just sat, straight and right.

She stood and went out to skate and as soon as she cleared the door he leaned down under the bunk and did something with the records. For a second I couldn't make it out, then I saw that he was changing the records on the turn-table. He took off the ones that were set up and put on a special stack and I thought right then that I had to get outside and get Willy to watch.

This was going to be something.

But before I went I saw Carl do a strange thing. He stood alone by his bunk and shrugged his shoulders down, almost like an exercise but not quite, either. It was more a getting ready kind of thing, like I'd seen a bullfighter doing in a movie before going out to face the bull. Getting his mind ready.

I went out to the hockey rink and skated onto the ice and got Willy just as the door to the warming house opened and Carl came out.

"Oh," Willy said, low and quiet. "He's . . . he's different, isn't he?"

I nodded. Other kids still played hockey but some of them had stopped and they were watching and on the other side a lot of the grownups had stopped to watch. Some of the little kids kept skating.

The music changed. The new records he had put on started to cycle through and the first one came on loud and strong, the sound ripping through the elms, coming out of the speakers with great booms and sharp edges.

It was a march. I had heard it once when the school band had done it but they messed it up the way they do and this time it sounded sort of the same because of the speakers.

Carl stopped just inside the gate on the ice,

stopped hard and strong and stood with his back straight and waited, waited until the people had stopped skating and Helen had turned from the right corner and saw him.

Then he made rigid movements, hard movements, forward and around, back and forth across the end of the rink and I couldn't figure it at first and I let my mind go easy and then I knew.

"He's young," Willy said, getting it at the same time. "He's young again. And in the army."

I nodded. "That's what I feel, too."

He moved with the strong movements until I thought he was done, thought he was going to leave, but no. He stopped then, with his back to Helen who was at the other end of the rink, watching him now. She was watching him openly, standing with her hands in the muff, her skates straight ahead.

The record changed and Carl turned and now it was a waltz and now he went around and down with those smooth movements that made me think of oil, made me think of smooth cream; he whirled around on the ice and let his arms go up and down like wings and it was as soft and beautiful as the first part had been hard.

He seemed to flow with the music, back and forth across the end of the rink and I let my mind follow the lines and I could see him showing something soft and beautiful and I thought of quiet places and whispers and happiness.

Other people at the rink were smiling and had light in their faces and Helen even had a small smile on her face, even and straight like the rest of her, but there, right across, a smile.

But still it wasn't about Carl, the dance. Still it was about something outside of him and he moved around and back and forth telling us, telling Helen about something beautiful that I couldn't make out until Willy nudged me.

"It's how he feels," he said. "About Helen. For Helen. It's about his feelings."

I nodded. "That, yes. But something else, too. Something about how he wants things to be, maybe. Something about how he wants his feelings to be."

And more. More in the cold blue of the white light coming down from the shining bulbs, in the scratchy sounds of the speakers and the chill of the rink and the steam from our breathing there was more. More in the music, more in the dance.

Carl danced back and forth across the end of the rink, twirling and looping, but never actually moving towards Helen, just back and forth, and she stood on her skates and watched, her eyes calm, not saying anything or doing anything.

There was not a way to know what she was

thinking. Not then, not so soon, but she watched and studied the dancing carefully and when he was finally done, down on the ice and back up to stand and the music was done and gone, she didn't turn away immediately.

She waited a moment, another moment, studying him as he moved and she knew that the dance was for her, was aimed at her, but when it was done she finally turned away and skated to the left, turned her shoulder away and I turned to Willy.

"That tears it. She isn't going to let him in. There's no telling what he'll do now. That's all he needed."

But if I thought Carl would be upset or fall apart I was wrong. He watched her skate away and rather than cave in his shoulders went back and his chin came out and he turned and went back into the warming house with strong steps.

And later, when she'd finished skating for the evening and came into the warming house both Willy and I were sitting there. Carl helped her off with her skates and she sat as straight and fine as any queen, all in the frayed wool tweed just straight and fine and Carl helped her off with her skates and on with her boots as if nothing had happened.

Watching him kneel that way I thought of King Arthur and the knights of the Round Table and the way the knights would kneel in front of the queen.

On the way home, walking in the dark with our skates over our sticks bouncing against our backs, Willy sighed.

"What's the matter?" I asked.

"That was so fine. Just so fine, the way he danced for her and she didn't care diddly about it."

"We don't know that. She just didn't show it. Maybe she's one of those who don't show things."

"There's no way to know, is there?"

And there wasn't anything to say to that so we just kept walking through the night until I got home and I fell asleep happy and didn't know or care why except that it had something to do with the way Carl had danced for Helen.

. : 15 : .

There came then such a strange time even some of the people who went through it, even some of the grownups, weren't sure if it really happened or if it was all a dream.

I'm not sure myself, and Willy just smiles when we talk about it so there's no telling what he thinks about it all.

Later, in the summer, I happened to be down at the old folks' home in the park by the river and I heard an older lady talking to one of the nurses. I was there to visit my grandma and she was still in treatment. And this lady said to the nurse that she'd heard somebody at the rinks had ". . . took to dance and had the joy put on him so that it like to run over on everybody."

And maybe that's how it was, maybe Carl had

the joy put on him and it ran over on us. But even so there came such a strange time that some of the people still whisper when they talk about it.

It started the very next night.

Helen came to skate and we were in the warming house because when Helen came we weren't about to be anywhere else. Not everybody, of course, just Willy and me and some of the other kids. The grownups were still kind of standoffish about it all.

Helen came in and Carl helped her with her skates, all over and down and gentle-firm, and then she went out on the rink, only I saw a small smile as she tiptoed through the door on her saw edges.

A short smile.

And when she was gone Carl took a long pull on the bottle and we went outside and when he came out we could tell he was drunk, really drunk. His eyes were misted over and there was a looseness to his arms and legs.

But it lifted off him like a blanket when he got on the ice. He came onto the rink with his arms out, then he bent them up at the elbows and it was not pretty and pretty at the same time, the way a falling bird can be both ugly and beautiful.

Up and over his head and he did a dance to

the music he'd set up, some crashing sounds of hard music that seemed to tear at the speakers.

Hard movements, sad movements, jagged lines that spun hard and around in fast and jerky circles that made everybody stop skating and stare, an ugly dance, a sad dance.

And Helen stopped and stared at him as well.

When he was done he went back into the warming house without looking back and I almost cried because I thought that was it, that was all of him and he was broken again and over and done.

That night Mom had to ask me something three times and Dad heard her repeat herself. I was sitting at the dining table and he was in his chair by the floor lamp and he put his paper down.

"Your mother asked you something."

It was another rule. You were supposed to listen. I tried to remember what she had said but couldn't and sat up. "I'm sorry. Something is bothering me."

"What?"

"Nothing, really. It's just something that's making me kind of sad and I was thinking about it and wasn't listening."

"What was it?" Mom asked.

I tried to think of a way to put it. "You know how Carl has taken over the rinks?"

Dad smiled. "The town talks about it all the time. What's so sad about that?"

"Not that. But he's dancing for this woman . . ."

"Helen. Yes. They talk about that, too. I've been meaning to come down and see it."

"But she doesn't care about him. She looks away from him. She's away from him more and more. And that's sad."

And Mom said something nice about how it was all just talk anyway and I smiled and thanked her but she didn't know because she hadn't seen it, had only heard about it. And the same for Dad. They couldn't know and I wanted it to be all right for Carl because of the incident with the B-17 model and it was going bad.

But I was wrong again.

The next day after school we hurried to the rinks in the coming dark, hurried to see what would happen and we played hockey for a time and about six Helen came.

Again Carl helped her with her skates and some of us watched and Helen nodded to him and he nodded to her and then she went out to skate.

This time Carl played the same hard music, and he danced the same crazy-hard dance, jerking around in the cold on the ice and I thought at first he was locked into doing that, had gone

crazy. But right at the end he did a graceful little swoop, a circle, a gentle move.

And back into the warming house and that
was the end of it for the night.

And the next night the same, a wild dance but
with a little more smooth on the end and we
knew then that Carl was working up to something, trying to reach Helen a new way.

"He could talk," I said to Willy, walking home
after the third night when we knew what he was
doing. "He has never said anything to her. He
could talk to her."

But Willy shook his head. "No. No he couldn't.
He could try but it wouldn't work like what he's
doing. He can't talk to her. Not yet."

And I was going to say something smart about
how Willy knew that but I didn't and I'm glad I
didn't.

The fourth night it was about half-and-half.
Half hard and wild and half beautiful and soft
except that there were many new things that he
did that fed one into another until it was all like
one dance. He came through the rink gate and
started around and down and up and by now
when he started everybody quit skating, quit
doing anything but watching.

Cleaner movements now, cleaner lines he
made and I felt my breath catch because this
was all new, all swoops and wide circles as he

followed his arms around and then off the rink.

And still nothing out of Helen. Except that just as he finished, her hand left the soft fur muff and came up towards her mouth, not all the way, just a short distance.

Then she skated away. Or almost.

Just at the other end she did a small circle with her skates, a small almost-flip-around. She stayed straight up and down and controlled, but it was a light thing to do and I turned back to Carl and his face lit just as he went into the warming house.

Ahh, I thought. Ahh, that was something to him, something good. And the small hairs on the back of my neck went up.

That was something good for Carl.

The end of it, the end of that fine thing and what Willy called the start of a new fine thing came the next night.

It was coming into late February and when the end of February comes in McKinley the weather can either be almost like spring or it can blow up a storm to freeze your water for you.

That night it was soft and almost warm, maybe twenty above, and no wind and light until six. It smelled of spring. I went home from school to deliver my papers and eat and get back to the rinks. Once a week I had this paper route and it didn't make me rich but it helped some and this time I hurried more than usual. We all wanted to be there to see what would happen. I went by Willy's and we got to the rinks about seven.

Nobody was skating. The hockey rink was full of kids but they were all standing, and on the quiet side everybody was off the ice and standing around the boards. Waiting.

We went into the warming house and saw Carl sitting on his bunk. Waiting.

But a new Carl.

Still with a flight jacket, still a little drunk, but he had clean pants and a clean shirt. And he'd shaved and I could see the red in his cheeks fresh and scrubbed and his hair was cut and combed and he sat straight and tall on the bunk.

He nodded to us, but then looked back to the door and continued to wait.

I took Willy's arm and we went outside without putting our skates on, went out to wait with the others by the rink.

When I stopped by the boards I looked out on the ice and there was something in the middle, something lying on the ice.

"What's that?" I asked Willy, who couldn't see it any better than I could. "What's that on the ice?"

He didn't answer and I was about ready to go

out and see when a grownup—I think it was old man Ekre from the drugstore—leaned over and whispered. "It's a flower."

"A flower?"

"Yes. It's a rose. A long-stemmed rose. He put it out there a few minutes ago."

And I didn't have to ask who put it on the ice.

At exactly seven Helen came walking down the side of the road, carrying her skates by the blade guards with one hand and the other one in the muff.

She didn't pay much attention to us except to pause and look at us standing there as she went into the warming house. In five or ten minutes she came back out—it seemed like hours—and she came to the rink with pleasant nods for the people standing by the boards.

Still, she went past and out to the ice and she knew what she was doing, knew then what it was all about because she skated once around the rink and didn't look down at the rose even though she skated right by it and it stuck out like a whole bush.

The music came on then, came on with a waltz and we all turned to the warming house to see Carl come out the door.

He walked to the rink in a straight line, laid out and down and stopped at the gate for only a second before stepping onto the ice.

Then he moved away from the gate on the blue of the ice in the warm evening, moved away in small circles and loops that went around with the music, made him part of the music and just when I thought he was done and saw everybody start to relax, just then he changed.

It was maybe that he went a little crazy or maybe he just found a place in me, in us, that was a little crazy, that he reached in and touched somehow, but he changed.

It was like he was younger. His dance got stronger and more powerful, with twirls that seemed to sparkle with light and fire, and around like that, around while Helen stood at the other end of the rink.

But it was different now. She wasn't standing to study, she was standing to wait, standing to see what he would do, could do for her as he moved around the ice.

Faster, faster all the time his feet just slicking along, his arms bending, his waist bending, faster and then to the rose.

He went to the rose and went past the rose and came back to it and pointed to it. Not with his arms or hand, not with his finger, he pointed to the rose somehow with the dance, somehow with all of everything he was he pointed to the rose and then away again.

Off to the side of the rink he danced, around,

and now I could hear his breathing coming hard and fast but still he didn't stop and back to the rose he came.

Again, with all of what he was doing he made me see the rose, made me watch the rose, and again away, away only not as far and back, and once more away and still back and again away and finally, chest heaving, arms hanging, shoulders bent, he stood about five feet from the rose.

Looking and down, at the rose and yet more too, the line of him not going to the rose so much as to the rose and back up to Helen, all in curves and we were frozen now, all of us, watching in the February night.

Waiting.

Waiting and for a second or two nothing happened. Then Willy nudged me and he didn't have to because I saw it, saw it coming.

"She's going to do it," Willy said.

Helen came, straight up and down, skating with her hands in the muff. She came across the ice and bent without seeming to bend and one hand come out of the muff and she picked up the rose—picked it up and looked at Carl, looked him right in the face, right in the eyes and she smiled and Carl answered the smile and we all breathed again. Carl moved off the ice to the warming house and she skated beside him and they went in and we all started skating and talking at once.

And I saw Carl many times after that, after he left the rinks. And maybe he was a little drunk but he was clean and happy when I saw him around town, and straight like maybe some of Helen rubbed off on him.

And I heard many things still later. I heard that Carl went crazy and should have been put in the state hospital and I heard that Helen had some part of her brain hurt many years before and I heard they moved into a house together and shared their government checks. I heard they couldn't be married because of something in Carl's life and I heard even later that Carl died of drink and Helen had to go to a special home to live and all of this happened in some other town they moved to and none of it, not one single thing of what I heard, makes any difference at all.

All that mattered then and all that matters now is that Helen stooped to pick up that rose.